*For Sigalle with love*

# Catch a Little Fox

Catch

# a *Little Fox*

## Variations on a Folk Rhyme

BEATRICE SCHENK DE REGNIERS

Pictures by BRINTON TURKLE

The Seabury Press · New York

First Seabury edition 1970. Library of Congress Catalog Card Number: 75-97036. Text copyright © 1968 by Beatrice Schenk de Regniers. Illustrations copyright © 1968 by Brinton Turkle. Printed in the U.S.A.

Oh a-hunting we will go.
A-hunting we will go.

1532352

We'll catch a little . . .

. . . fox
and put him in a box

and never let him go.

Oh a-hunting we will go.
A-hunting we will go.

We'll catch a little . . .

. . . frog
and put him in a log

and never let him go.

Oh a-hunting we will go.
A-hunting we will go.

We'll catch a little . . .

. . . cat
and put him in a hat

and never let him go.

Oh a-hunting we will go.
A-hunting we will go.

We'll catch a little . . .

. . . mouse
and put him in a house

and never let him go.

Oh a-hunting we will go.
A-hunting we will go.

We'll catch a little . . .

. . . dragon
and put him in a wagon

and never let him go.

Oh a-hunting we will go.
A-hunting WE will go.

We'll put them in a ring
and listen to them sing

1532352

Oh a - hunt - ing we will go. A - hunt - ing we will go. We'll

catch a lit - tle fox and put him in a box and nev - er let him go.

. . . and then we'll let them go.

4582